The Story of the Treasure Seekers

'Let's be quiet for ten minutes. How can we find treasure? We must each think about that. Then we'll try all our ideas, one after the other.'

The six Bastable children want to be rich again. Their father had money before, but now they are poor. So they start to look for treasure.

When they look for treasure, they meet many interesting people, and a lot of exciting things happen. But will they find any treasure? Will their family one day be rich again? Who is the man from India, and can he help?

Edith Nesbit was born in London in 1858. She was a very beautiful woman, and she worked hard because she wanted the world to be a better place. She and her husband, Hubert Bland, together tried to help poor people and workers in England.

Edith did not start to write children's stories until she was quite old. *The Story of the Treasure Seekers* was her first children's book; she wrote it in 1899. She remembered the things she did when she was a child, and this always helped her to write her stories.

She wrote very many books for children. A famous book of hers is *The Railway Children*, which is a Penguin Reader too.

The Story of
the Treasure Seekers

E. NESBIT

Level 2

Retold by Robin Waterfield
Series Editors: Andy Hopkins and Jocelyn Potter

Addison Wesley Longman Limited
Edinburgh Gate, Harlow,
Essex CM20 2JE, England
and Associated Companies throughout the world.

ISBN 0 582 40153 4

First published 1899
This adaptation first published by Penguin Books 1997
This edition first published 1998

Text copyright © Robin Waterfield 1997
Illustrations copyright © Kay Dixey 1997
All rights reserved

The moral right of the adapter and of the illustrator has been asserted

Typeset by RefineCatch Limited, Bungay, Suffolk
Set in 11/14pt Lasercomp Bembo
Printed in Spain by Mateu Cromo, S.A. Pinto (Madrid)

Published by Addison Wesley Longman Limited in association with
Penguin Books Ltd., both companies being subsidiaries of Pearson Plc

Dictionary words:

● Some words in this book are darker black than others. Look them up in your dictionary or try to understand them without a dictionary first, and then look them up later.

Before you read:

1 Write down the words for five different *treasures*. Use your dictionary.
2 Look at the first six pictures in this book.
  a When do you think the story happened?
  b In which country or city do you think it happened?
  c Which picture shows you the most important people in the story?
3 Look at the last two pictures. How do you think the story finishes – happily or sadly?

Chapter One

One day we started to try to look for treasure. You will see that we tried very hard to find it.

There are six children in our family, and then there is Father. Our mother is dead. I will not talk about her. We all loved her, so it is difficult to talk about her. We live in Lewisham Road in London. We are the Bastables.

Dora is the oldest, then there is Oswald – that's me. Then Dicky is next, then Alice and Noel, who were born at the same time. After them comes Horace Octavius, who is my youngest brother. Everybody calls him H.O.

We have a problem. Father lost all his money. His **business** went wrong. We weren't always **poor**, but now we are poor. Now we do not have nice things, and Father does not give us money, and all the chairs and plates and things in the house are old. And we do not go to school now.

'Father never tells us that we are poor,' Dora said one day. 'But we all know.'

'We must do something,' said Alice.

'Yes – but what can we do?' asked Dicky.

'Let's read all our books again,' said Noel. 'We'll get a lot of **ideas** out of them.' Noel wrote **poems**, and always read books.

Then Dicky said, 'Let's be quiet for ten minutes. How can we find treasure? We must each think about that. Then we'll try all our ideas, one after the other.'

After ten minutes, we all started to talk at the same time, but Dora told us to be quiet.

I spoke first. 'We must **save** someone from danger. He'll give us a lot of money, because he'll be very happy with us.'

There are six children in our family.

'But there's no danger near here,' said Dora. 'What do *you* think, Alice?'

'Noel must find a **princess** and **marry** her,' said Alice.

'I don't want to marry a princess,' said Noel. 'I want to put my poems in a book. People will buy the book, and then we'll be rich.'

'That's a bad idea,' said Dicky. 'Who's going to buy *your* poems? We must start a business, I think. We start with a little money. We buy some things and sell them for more money. It's easy. We'll soon be rich.'

'But we have no money to buy the things,' Noel said.

H.O. said, 'Let's be **robbers** and take money from people.'

'That's a bad thing to do,' said Dora, 'but in books people always find money in the **ground**. Some people **hide** their money in the ground, and other people find it. So we must **dig** for money. Let's do it now, because I'm the oldest.'

Chapter Two

We started to dig in the garden. It was hard work, because the ground was very hard. We dug and dug and dug, but we found nothing.

Soon Albert came from the next house. We like his **uncle** who lives there, but we do not like Albert very much. But his father is dead, so we are sorry for him, and we try to be friendly. Albert's uncle writes books, and when he talks children can understand him.

'What are you doing?' Albert asked.

'We're digging for treasure,' said Alice. 'You can help us.'

Albert laughed and said, 'You won't find any treasure in your garden.'

Albert is not very good at games. He does not read many books, so he does not have many ideas.

3

But I said, 'Come and dig. You can have some of the treasure when we find it.'

'I don't want to dig,' said Albert. 'I want to go and have my tea.'

But Alice asked him nicely, and then he came and started digging. We all worked too. Pincher, our dog, tried to dig near us.

Then Albert fell in the **hole** and the ground fell on him. We could see only his head. We tried to get him out, but we could not. He cried and cried. Dicky went to get Albert's uncle from the next house.

'Why are you crying?' Albert's uncle asked when he came.

'I can't get out,' Albert said.

'Stop crying, please,' said his uncle.

'We're trying to find treasure,' Alice said. 'I think we were close.'

Albert's uncle started digging Albert out of the ground. When he pulled him out, he was all dirty.

'Look, look!' said Albert's uncle. 'You were right! You were close to some treasure! There it is in the hole!'

He sat down and took something out of the hole. We all ran and looked. And there, in his hand, was one pound.

'There was no money in the hole before,' Dora said, and looked at Albert's uncle.

'You *are* lucky,' said Albert's uncle. 'The first time you look for treasure, you find some!'

Chapter Three

'With this money we can start a business,' said Dicky.

'No,' said Dora, 'We must get much more first.'

'And I want to buy a pencil,' said Noel.

We all wanted to buy things. Soon we had only ten pence.

'We found some treasure,' I said, 'but we aren't rich. What are we going to do next?'

Then Albert fell in the hole. We could see only his head.
He cried and cried.

'Let's take my poems to a newspaper,' Noel said. 'I think they'll buy them for a lot of money.'

We wrote six of Noel's poems on some paper. Then he and I took the train into London. I went with him, because I am older.

A woman sat down near us in the train. We started talking to her. 'This is my brother Noel,' I said. 'We're going to London to sell his poems to a newspaper. We want to help our father. He has no money.'

'I'm very interested,' the woman said. 'I write poems too, you know. I'm always happy to meet a writer of poems. My name is Mrs Leslie. Can I read your poems, Noel? I will show you some of my poems too.'

She read Noel's poems. 'I like them a lot,' she said. 'I think you'll be a famous writer of poems one day.'

When the train stopped, she tried to give us some money.

'No, thank you,' I said. 'We mustn't take money from people when we don't know them.'

'You're right,' said the woman. 'But when you get home, tell your father my name. You can send the money back to me or have it. Your father will tell you what you must do.'

We said goodbye and left the train. All the newspapers have their offices on Fleet Street, so we went there. We walked into the first newspaper office in the street.

'What do you two boys want?' asked a man.

'We want your newspaper to buy Noel's poems,' I said.

'Wait here,' said the man. We sat down on chairs near the front door. The man went away. We waited a long time. Then a different man came and smiled at us. He had a moustache.

'The boss of the newspaper can't see you now,' he said. 'Why are you here?'

Noel was quite angry. 'Tell him that I'm a friend of Mrs Leslie,' he said. 'I write poems too, and I want him to buy my poems.'

She read Noel's poems. 'I like them a lot,' she said.

The man with the moustache went away again. Soon he came back. 'He'll see you now,' he said. He smiled again.

We went with him up into the office. We came to a big room, and there was the boss.

'You're friends of Mrs Leslie?' he said.

'Yes,' I said. 'She gave us some money, so we must be friends.'

'Do you write the poems?' he asked me.

'No. This is my brother Noel. He writes the poems.' Why did he think it was me? I am strong, not weak, because I play outside and do not stay inside and read books.

Noel gave him the poems. The newspaper boss started to read them. He read one of them, and then he turned his head away. We could not see his face. At home that evening Noel said, 'The man thought my poems were sad, I think, and he didn't want us to see him sad.'

He read all the poems, and then he said, 'I like your poems very much, young man. How much do you want me to pay for them?'

Noel was very happy. 'Please give me a lot,' he said. 'It's import-ant. Our father is poor now, and we're trying to get a lot of money for him and our family.'

'That's a very good thing to do,' the man said. 'But first, do you want some tea?'

We sat and drank a cup of tea with the newspaper man, and then he gave Noel a pound for his poems. Noel went red and then white. He could not say anything, so I said, 'Thank you very much. You're very good.'

'Go home now,' the man said, 'and bring me some more poems in about ten years. I'm only taking these poems now because I like them, but this newspaper doesn't usually buy poems.'

'What do you put in your newspaper?' I asked.

'Oh, stories about famous people,' he answered. 'Do you know any?'

'We often see Lord Tottenham in the park,' I said. 'He talks

We sat and drank a cup of tea with the newspaper man.

when there's nobody there. Do you want to put that in your newspaper?'

'Yes, that's very good,' the man said. 'Thank you. I'll give you some more money for that. Here you are.'

Noel quickly wrote a poem about the newspaper man and gave it to him. He liked it a lot. Then we all said goodbye. And home we went with more than a pound!

But the man never put Noel's poems in his newspaper. Much later we saw a story in a different newspaper, and Noel's poems were in the story. The story was about two boys. They wanted to sell poems to a newspaper. 'The writer of the story is laughing at the boys,' I said, but Noel was happy. His poems were in a newspaper.

Chapter Four

We did not look for the princess, but we found her. And Noel did marry her! But we did not get any treasure from it.

We often played in Greenwich Park. The park is very big and there are always new things to see. One day in the park Alice said, 'Let's play that we're hungry people in the old days and we're looking for an animal to eat.'

'I'll be the animal,' Noel said.

Noel hid in the trees, and we followed him and tried to find him. 'Look!' said Dora. 'This is a new place. There's a door over there.'

The door was open. Noel was inside, in a garden. Next to him was a little girl.

'Who are you?' said the little girl.

'I'm a famous fighter,' said Noel. He forgot that he was an animal.

'And I'm a princess,' said the little girl. We liked her a lot. She was very good at games. 'Are you all famous fighters too?' she asked us. She spoke English, but she was not from England.

'I'm a famous fighter,' said Noel.
'And I'm a princess,' said the little girl.

'Yes,' we said.

'Where is your **coach**?' asked the girl. 'How did you come here?'

'We don't have a coach,' I said. 'We walked through the park.'

'What's your name?' Dicky asked.

She started to tell us her name, and when she started, it was a long time before she stopped. The first names were Pauline, Alexandra and Alice; Mary was in there, and Victoria was too – we all heard Victoria. The last names were Hildegarde Cunigonde or something, Princess of some place.

'She has fifty names!' H.O. said.

'No, only eighteen,' said Dicky.

'Why are you here in England?' Dora asked.

'We're visiting Queen Victoria,' said the little girl. She was *very* good at games.

'Will you play with us in the park?' I asked.

'I mustn't go into the park,' she said sadly. 'I want to climb trees, but I mustn't get dirty and they say it's dangerous for a princess.'

'We must go home soon,' Noel said, 'so let's marry now.'

The little girl did not understand, but then she did, and Noel married her. Then we played some other games. She liked to play 'Catch'. She ran after Dicky, but then she suddenly stopped. Her face was sad. We saw two old women with small mouths and dark hair.

'Pauline!' said one of the women. 'Who are these children?'

'They're famous fighters,' said the little girl.

'No, they're not,' said the woman. 'They're only children.'

'But I'm happy to play with them,' said the little girl, and she ran to us.

'Wilson,' said the woman, 'carry the princess inside the house.'

And the other woman came and caught the little girl, and carried her away. Then the first woman said, 'Go away now, or I'll call the police!'

So we went back to the park. 'She *was* a princess!' Dora said.

Back home we had bread and butter for tea. 'I want to give her some,' Noel said. 'It's very good, and she's as beautiful as the day.'

Chapter Five

We used nearly all the money from Noel's poems on things for Father's birthday, so we could not start a business, and soon we were poor again.

But then Dora went away to stay with our uncle in Stroud for a holiday.

'Now we can be robbers,' said H.O. 'Dora says it's wrong to be robbers, but now she isn't here.'

So we went into the park to be robbers. We hid behind some trees and waited for someone to come. We waited a long time, but nobody came.

After two hours Noel said, 'Let's go home for tea. I'm cold.'

'Me too!' said Alice.

But I said, 'Quiet! Somebody's coming through the trees!'

We hid carefully and then jumped out when the walker was close. It was only Albert from the house next to us. He was very afraid when we jumped out from behind the trees.

We caught him and took him to our house. He didn't want to play. 'I want to go home,' he said.

'We're dangerous robbers,' said H.O. 'You can go home only when your family gives us some money. You're our **prisoner**.'

'But you can have some of our tea,' I said. And when we had our tea, we gave the prisoner some too. But first we made a prison out of chairs and boxes and things.

After tea we got some paper and wrote a letter to Albert's family. The letter said: 'Albert Morrison is a prisoner of some robbers. You can have him back when you pay us three thousand pounds.'

13

We hid carefully and then jumped out when the walker was close.
It was only Albert from the house next to us.

H.O. took the letter to Mrs Morrison. Soon he came back with Albert's uncle.

'Oh, no!' said Albert's uncle. 'What's this? You're a prisoner of dangerous robbers! Oh, what can I do?'

'I didn't want to play,' Albert said, 'but they put me in this prison.'

'It's a very nice prison,' Albert's uncle said. 'Perhaps I'll leave you there.'

Albert began to cry.

'Don't cry, boy,' said Albert's uncle. 'But I don't have three thousand pounds. It's a lot of money.'

'What do you have?' I asked.

'Only eight pence, I'm afraid,' he said. 'Will you take that?'

'Yes,' I said.

'Thank you very much,' said Alice, when he gave her the money. 'But it was only a game. Do you want to give us the money?'

'Yes, I do,' said Albert's uncle.

So we opened the prison and Albert went home. Then Albert's uncle sat down in a chair near the fire.

'You know, children,' he said, 'it's good to play games, and I like Albert to play with you too. It's good for him. But you must be careful. Did you think about Albert's mother? When Albert is away from home for a long time, perhaps she'll think that something bad is happening to him. Today it was OK, but you must be careful. Do you understand?'

He wasn't very angry, but he wanted to say these things.

Nobody said anything. Then Alice spoke. Girls often say things when we can't say them. She put her hand on Albert's uncle's hand and said, 'We're very, very sorry. We didn't think about his mother. We try hard not to think about other people's mothers because . . .'

Then we heard Father's key in the door. Albert's uncle smiled. We all ran down to meet Father.

Alice put her hand on Albert's uncle's hand and said,
'We're very, very sorry.'

Chapter Six

'I'm right,' I said. 'I know I'm right. We must save someone from danger, and he'll give us a lot of money.'

'Yes, let's try Oswald's idea,' Dicky said. 'We're trying all the other ideas, so we must try Oswald's bad idea too.'

'It's not a bad idea,' I said. 'We'll be rich. You'll see.'

'We must save Lord Tottenham,' Alice said. 'He's rich, and he walks in the park every day.'

'But when is he in danger?' Dicky asked. Nobody could answer that.

'I know,' I said. 'Dora, Dicky and Noel can be robbers, and Alice, H.O. and I can save Lord Tottenham from the robbers.'

'It's wrong to be robbers,' Dora said, so we tried to think of a different idea.

Then Alice said, 'What about Pincher?'

'You're right,' we said.

Pincher is a very good dog. When we tell him to get something, he takes it and doesn't open his mouth.

'But this is wrong too,' said Dora. 'I won't play this game. It's a mistake.' So she did not come with us.

'Alice,' I said, 'you and H.O. must hide behind some trees in the park. When Lord Tottenham walks close to the trees, you must tell Pincher to catch him. Then Noel, Dicky and I will save him. And he'll say, "Thank you, thank you. That dog was very dangerous. Can I give you something?" Then we'll be rich and famous, and Father will never be poor again.'

So we went to the park and waited near the road. 'There's Lord Tottenham,' Dicky said after about twenty minutes.

'Quickly,' I said to Alice and H.O. 'Go and hide.'

They hid behind the trees with Pincher. Noel, Dicky and I

17

waited behind some other trees. When Lord Tottenham walked close to Alice and H.O., suddenly Pincher ran out.

'Look out!' I called, but Pincher took Lord Tottenham's trousers in his teeth.

Lord Tottenham jumped up and down. 'Help! Help!' he said. But Pincher's teeth were strong.

We ran over to him. When we got there I stopped and said, 'Dicky, we must save this good old man.'

' "Good old man"?' said Lord Tottenham. 'Get this dog off me!'

'It's a dangerous job,' I said, 'but we must do it.'

'Quick!' said Noel. 'You must save the old man from danger now!'

'Stop jumping, old man!' I said. 'I'll try to help.'

Then I quietly said to Pincher, 'Open your mouth, Pincher.'

Pincher opened his mouth and Lord Tottenham moved away. 'Thank you very much,' he said. 'Here's something for you.' And he got a pound out of his coat.

'I was right!' I thought. 'We'll be rich!' But then I thought: 'No, the old man was afraid. It was wrong. I won't take his money.'

Then Pincher jumped up at me. He was happy to see me. Lord Tottenham opened his eyes and said, 'The dog knows you!'

I turned and started to walk away quickly, but Lord Tottenham caught Noel and said, 'No, you don't. What's happening here?'

Alice loves Noel more than anyone, and when she saw him in Lord Tottenham's hands, she ran out from behind the tree.

'So there are more of you?' Lord Tottenham said. Then H.O. came out too.

'Is that all?' asked Lord Tottenham.

'Yes,' H.O. said. 'There are only five of us today.'

Lord Tottenham turned and began to walk away.

'Where are you going?' I asked.

'To the police!' he said.

'Oh, but don't take Noel,' said Dicky. 'He's not strong.'

Lord Tottenham jumped up and down. 'Help! Help!' he said.

Lord Tottenham looked at Noel. Noel's face was all white. He stopped walking and we all sat down.

'You're bad children,' he said. 'You nearly took one pound from me.'

'Yes,' I said, 'I know now that we were wrong. I didn't want your money.'

'Why did you do it?' asked Lord Tottenham.

'We wanted money for our family,' I said. 'Our father's business went wrong and we want to help him. All the books say that when you save an old man from danger, he'll want you to be his son, or he'll give you money or start a business for you. But there was no danger here, so we used Pincher.'

'But some people are weak and are afraid of dogs,' said Lord Tottenham. 'You can kill people.'

We all started to cry.

'I can see that you're all sorry,' he said. 'Perhaps this will be a lesson to you. We'll say no more about it. I'm an old man now, but I was young before.'

Then Alice moved close to him and put her hand on his arm. 'I think you're very good,' she said. 'We're very, very sorry. When children do things in books, it's always OK. It isn't the same for us. And I know Oswald didn't want to take the money. I thought it was bad, and he did too.'

Lord Tottenham stood up and said, 'Always remember: never do wrong!'

'We'll remember,' we said. Then he took off his hat to us, and we took off ours, and he went away, and we went home. Dora said, 'I told you!'

We didn't go to the park for a week after that, but then we went and waited for Lord Tottenham. When he came, Alice said, 'Please, Lord Tottenham, here are some things for you.' And Noel gave him a poem, H.O. and I gave him our best knife, Alice gave him some flowers, and Dicky gave him a book.

Alice said, 'Please, Lord Tottenham, here are some things for you.'

Lord Tottenham liked the things. 'Thank you very much,' he said.

Now, when we meet him in the park, he takes off his hat to us and smiles, so I think we are friends.

Chapter Seven

One Saturday we were all up in Noel's bedroom in the evening, after dinner. It was cold outside, and there was a warm fire in the room.

'Listen,' I said. 'I heard the front door.'

'Yes,' Dora said, 'Father is going out this evening. The cook is out too; she says that she can find cheap food on Saturday nights. So there's nobody in the house, only us.'

We cooked some food on the fire and talked about robbers. Dicky said, 'It must be very interesting. Robbers can rob from rich people and give things to poor people.'

Dora said, 'It's wrong to be a robber.'

'Yes,' said Alice, 'a robber is always unhappy, I think. First he takes other people's money and hides it under his bed. Then how can he sleep? He always thinks that policemen and detectives are coming to his house.'

'Perhaps there's a robber in the house now,' said Alice. 'What will you do to him?'

Dicky and I didn't answer, but Noel said, 'First I'll ask him to go away . . .'

Before Noel stopped talking, we all heard a noise. We did not *think* it; there *was* a noise. Someone moved a chair in the house. But there was nobody in the house, only us!

H.O. and Alice and Dora looked at Dicky and me. Everyone was quite white. 'What are you going to do?' Dora asked quietly.

'I don't think it's a robber,' Noel said, but he was afraid.

'What are we going to do? Where's Father?' Dora said.

'Perhaps we can open the window and call the police,' Alice said.

'I think it's a cat,' I said. ' Let's go down and see.'

The girls were happy at the idea that it was a cat, but they did not want to go down and see. But Dicky said, 'I'll come with you.'

H.O. said, '*Is* it a cat?'

'Stay here with the girls,' I said. 'Dicky and I will go and see.'

We quietly opened the door of the bedroom. We stood there and listened for a very long time, but we heard nothing. Then I told Dicky to get his gun from his cupboard. We use the gun for our fighting in the park. When Dicky brought it, I took it, because I am the oldest.

'Do you think it *is* a cat?' Dicky asked.

'No,' I said.

I was afraid, but I went slowly down with Dicky. Alice and H.O. followed us. We saw light under the door to Father's room. I was happy. 'Robbers only like the dark,' I thought. 'This isn't a robber.'

But I wanted the others to think there was a robber, so with the gun in my hand I said, 'Come on, Dicky!' I walked into the room . . . and there was a robber! There was no mistake about it. He stood near the door of the cupboard, and the cupboard was open. There was nothing expensive in the cupboard, but a robber doesn't know these things.

'Put your hands up,' I said.

The robber put his hands up. 'Don't use your gun,' he said. 'How many of you are there?'

'There are a lot of us,' Dicky said. 'Do you have a gun or a knife?'

'No, nothing,' answered the robber.

We looked at the robber. He was not the same as robbers in books. He wore a good jacket and trousers. He had a thin face and blue eyes. He was clean, and as old as our father.

'Now I'm your prisoner,' he said. 'What are you going to do with me? Will you take me to the police?'

'Now I'm your prisoner. What are you going to do with me?'

Alice and the others were in the room too by now. They looked at the robber with open mouths.

'Will you try to run away?' Alice asked.

'No,' said the robber.

'Then we won't call the police,' she said. 'We'll wait for our Father.'

The robber sat down in a chair. 'I wasn't always a robber,' he said. 'I had a better job before. I don't want to be a prisoner, but you're very clever so I'm sorry to be your prisoner. How did you know I was in the house?'

We told him, and then we talked for a long time. He told us about his years at sea, on ships. It was very exciting. 'It's not always nice and exciting,' he said. 'When the weather's bad, it's not good at sea. But usually it's good. You see the world, you hear different languages and you meet many interesting people.'

'But before you were at sea, what did you do?' asked Dora. 'Did you have a different job?'

'No,' he said. 'I went to a good school – Eton.'

'That was my father's school,' H.O. began to say, but Dicky said, 'We tried to be robbers too, but our only prisoner was Albert from the house next to us.'

Then suddenly our robber put up his hand and told us to be quiet. 'What's that noise?' he said.

We listened and we heard a noise from the kitchen.

'Someone is trying to open the window,' he said. 'Give me that gun. There *is* a robber now, and no mistake about it.'

'The gun is only for games,' I said, when I gave it to him.

Then we heard a different noise. 'Now he's opening the window and climbing inside,' said the robber quietly. 'You must stay here, children. I'll go down and catch the robber.'

But Dicky and I wanted to go with him. We waited outside the kitchen door, with the others behind us. We were all very excited. 'Do you think our robber is going to climb out of the window and run home?' I asked Dicky.

'No,' said Dicky. 'He's friendly. I like him.'

'I do too,' I said. And we were right.

Our robber pushed the kitchen door open suddenly and ran in with the gun. 'Stop!' he called. 'Put up your hands!'

We looked round the door. There was a man in the kitchen. He was quite different from our robber. He had dark hair and a dirty face, and his coat and trousers had holes in them. He was poor. He put up his hands. 'OK, OK, boss!' he said. 'Don't use that gun! I'll be good.'

'Oswald,' our robber said to me, 'we must call the police.'

'No,' said the poor robber, 'don't do that! I don't always rob houses, but I have no money and my children at home are very hungry. I have two children, a boy and a girl. What can I do? I can't find a job. But I'll stop being a robber. I'm not very good at it.'

'No, you're not,' said our robber. 'We heard a lot of noise.'

'Oh, don't call the police,' said Alice. 'He has a daughter at home. What will she do without her father, when he's in prison?'

'No,' said our robber, 'he must go to prison. I don't think he has a daughter at home.'

'Ask your father to be nice, little girl,' said the robber to Alice. 'Then he won't call the police.'

'You must never come back here again,' said Alice.

'I won't,' said the man.

'And you must not rob again,' said Alice.

'I never will again,' he said.

Then Alice said to our robber, 'I think he'll be good now. Don't call the police, please.'

'No,' said our robber. 'That's wrong. We must wait for your father, and then he or I will call the police.'

'But you're a robber too,' said H.O. 'It isn't right. Why will you call the police for *him*, when we didn't call the police for you?'

'Ha! So you're a robber too,' said the poor robber. He jumped at our robber and pushed the gun out of his hand. Then he ran over to

26

He jumped at our robber and pushed the gun out of his hand.

the window and climbed out of it, before anybody could do anything. When he was outside, he turned and said to Alice, 'I'll give your love to my wife and children, little girl!' Then he ran away into the night.

We closed the window and went back up to Father's room. 'This is a very interesting night,' said our robber.

'Yes,' said Dicky. 'We never had a more exciting time.'

Then we heard a noise. It was Father's key in the front door.

'Quick! Hide!' said Alice. 'You're a nice man. I don't want Father to call the police. I don't want you to go to prison!'

But Father was in the house by now. 'Where are you, Foulkes?' he called. 'I've got the . . .' Then he stopped when he saw us. 'What are you doing, children?'

Nobody said anything.

Then Father said, 'Foulkes, were the children bad?'

'No, no,' our robber said. 'I'm not Foulkes. I'm a robber. I'm the prisoner of these children. They're very good. They tried to save your house when you were out.'

Then we began to understand. 'You're playing a game,' Dora said.

Then our robber said to us, 'I'm not a robber. I'm an old friend of your father. I came after dinner, and your father went out to get a letter for me from some people. My son is ill, and with this letter I can go and see a good doctor. This doctor will help my son. I waited in your father's room. I wanted to get the letter from your father when he came back.'

We could not say anything.

Our robber told Father about the other robber, and Father said, 'You had an exciting night!'

Then he went and got some food from the kitchen, and we ate it there in his room with our fingers, which was most unusual. Father was very happy. 'When was Father last happy?' I thought. 'When will he be happy again?'

Chapter Eight

Father says that Noel's shoes make a noise on the floor. 'Your uncle from India is coming to visit me tonight, children,' he said. 'I want you to be very quiet. He and I must talk about some business.' So we took Noel's shoes off, but there were other noises in the house. Eliza, our cook, makes a lot of noise in the kitchen. 'There I was,' she told us later. 'I'm making dinner, and trying to be quick, and I break two plates!'

'Listen to all that noise!' the Indian Uncle said when he arrived. Father took him into his room. 'But he isn't dark,' Noel said. 'Indians are dark. He's brown from the sun, that's all.' He had a white moustache too.

I don't think the dinner was very nice. Our cook is not very good. We sat on the floor near our bedrooms and watched. The Indian Uncle came out of Father's room and got something from his coat. It was a box of cigars. 'That food wasn't very good!' he said.

We didn't try to hear, but we did hear him, because he did not talk quietly. We heard him and Father from inside the room too.

'It's a good business,' Father said. 'With a little more money, it will be a *very* good business.'

'You're wrong,' said the uncle. 'What does the business want? New men, not more money.'

'It's difficult for me to talk about it,' Father said sadly. 'Let's not talk about it again.'

After that they talked about other things, and we went to our playroom.

'Now I understand,' Noel said. 'Father is giving the Indian Uncle dinner because he's poor. Father's trying to help him.'

'Yes,' said Alice. 'So Father didn't want us to come to dinner,

29

We sat on the floor near our bedrooms and watched.

because the Indian Uncle is poor. He doesn't like other people to know that he's poor.'

'I'm sorry that the dinner was bad,' said Dora.

'Yes,' I said. 'Perhaps the poor Indian doesn't eat meat every day. Then he comes to our house for dinner and Eliza cooks the meat badly.'

'Let's ask the poor Indian to come to lunch with us tomorrow,' Alice said.

'That's a good idea,' we all said.

'You younger children must go to bed,' I said. 'We'll wait and talk to the poor Indian. We'll tell you all about it tomorrow.'

I waited by the back door. Dicky waited up by our bedrooms. 'When the uncle is going to leave,' I said, 'you must make a noise. Then I'll go round the outside of the house. I'll meet him by the front door and talk to him.'

So when the poor Indian left, I met him at the front of the house. 'Good evening, Uncle,' I said.

He looked at me. He didn't say anything. 'Perhaps boys are not always nice to poor people,' I thought.

'Good evening, Uncle,' I said again.

'It's late, young man,' he said. 'Why are you out of bed?'

'You had dinner with my father,' I said. 'I know the dinner wasn't good, and I'm sorry, because you're poor and you want a good dinner. So will you come and have lunch with us tomorrow in our playroom? We don't think it's wrong to be poor.'

'And what's *your* name?' he asked.

'Oswald Bastable,' I said.

'So, Oswald Bastable, yes, I will come to have lunch with you tomorrow. Thank you very much. Good night to you. I'll come at one o'clock. Is that all right?'

'Yes,' I said. 'Good night.'

Then I went in and told Dicky and Dora. 'We mustn't tell Father,' I said. 'He gave the Indian Uncle a bad dinner, but we'll give him a good lunch. Father mustn't know that we give people food better than his.'

The next day we did tell Eliza. 'A friend is coming for lunch,' we said. 'Can you make him all the nicest things?'

'She thinks it's Albert from the next house,' I said quietly to Dora.

At one o'clock the Indian Uncle arrived. I helped him to take off his coat, and then I took him up to our playroom. We usually had lunch there.

'Hello,' he said to everyone when he came in. 'How old are you?' We told him. 'And what school do you go to?'

'We're on holiday these days,' said Dora. He was unhappy about that. Then Eliza brought the food. The food was nice; she cooked the meat and the vegetables well. But nobody said anything. What could we say? 'Oh no,' I thought. 'This is going to be difficult. Nobody will say anything.'

Then Alice said, 'Do you want a play-lunch, Uncle?'

And he said, 'Play-lunch? Yes, let's have a play-lunch.'

We were happy. 'It's going to be OK,' I thought.

'How do we play?' the Uncle asked.

We showed him. 'We're fighters in Africa,' Alice said. 'The meat is an animal. We kill the animal and then we eat it.'

So we all killed the meat with our knives and things. We cut the meat and cooked it some more on the fire. 'This meat is very good,' said the Indian Uncle. But his meat was a little black from the fire.

After the meat we had fruit. 'What do we do with this?' asked the uncle.

'We get it from the trees,' Noel said, 'before we can eat it.'

The Indian Uncle climbed on to a chair and got the fruit from a tree. Then he robbed some more food from a ship.

After lunch, I asked him, 'Was that good? Was it better than last night?'

And the Indian Uncle said, 'I never had a better lunch.'

32

So we all killed the meat with our knives and things.

He smoked a cigar and told us about all the animals in India. We liked him very much.

'Now I must go,' he said. Alice kicked me under the table. I remembered.

'Wait,' I said. 'You're poor. We have a little money. Please, will you take this money?' And I showed him a sixpence and a threepence.

'I'll take the threepence,' he said. 'Where did you get the money for the lunch? Does your father give you money?'

'No,' we said. 'Father doesn't give us money now. We're treasure-seekers. We try to find treasure, and sometimes we do find a little. Father is poor, you see, so we try to help him.'

We told the Indian Uncle about Mrs Leslie and Noel's poems, and the treasure in the hole in the garden, and Lord Tottenham, and the princess. He asked a lot of questions. When he went away he said, 'Children, thank you very much. I had a very good time. Perhaps one day the poor Indian will ask all of you to dinner.'

'Thank you,' I said, 'and you can buy cheap food for our dinner. We don't always have expensive food.' I said this because he was poor.

The next day a large coach drove down the road outside our house. 'Do you think it will stop here?' I said. 'No, nobody stops here.'

But the coach did stop at our house! There were a lot of boxes on top, and the driver started to get the boxes down and to bring them into the house. Then somebody's foot and leg began to come out of the coach.

'It's the poor Indian!' said Noel.

'Yes, it is!' Dora said.

Eliza opened the front door. Then the poor Indian said to Father, 'Dick, I had lunch with your children yesterday. They're nice children. When I look at Dora, I remember your wife, Jane. And young Oswald . . .'

But the coach did stop at our house! There were a lot of boxes on top.

Then he and Father went into Father's room, and we couldn't hear anything more. So we went down and looked at the boxes. There were big ones and small ones.

'Perhaps the Indian Uncle is coming to stay with us,' said Dicky.

When they came out of Father's room, we asked him, 'Are these boxes yours?'

'No,' he said, 'they are for you. I told a – what can I say? – a *friend* about you, and he gave me a lot of things. Some of them are from India. You can have them all.'

We took the boxes up to our playroom. Father and the Indian Uncle came too. We opened all the boxes. There was a train for Dicky and me, a lot of books, games, pictures and fruit. Every box had beautiful things in it.

Father looked at everything. The uncle said, 'My . . . er . . . friend gave you these, Dick.' And he gave Father a paper-knife and a box of cigars.

So we found some treasure; these boxes were treasure.

The Indian Uncle often visited us after that, and he always brought something from his friend. One day he said, 'Do you remember that I wanted you to have dinner with me? You can all come on Christmas Day. Will you come?'

'Yes,' we said. 'Can we go, Father?'

'Yes,' he said. 'I'm coming too.'

Father was always happy now. Perhaps Uncle's friend gave him some money for his business, because we usually had a little money now.

On Christmas Day we took two coaches to the Indian Uncle's house. 'Where does he live?' Alice asked. 'In one of these poor houses?'

We went past the poor houses and drove to a very big house near the park. The coaches stopped there. 'Perhaps he works here,' I thought.

We drove to a very big house near the park.
The coaches stopped there.

But no – the house was his. He lived there. He was not a poor Indian; he was very rich. For Christmas he gave each of us a watch.

After lunch, Uncle said, 'Some friends are coming to visit us this afternoon.' And in came Lord Tottenham, Mrs Leslie, Albert's uncle – and Albert – and best of all Mr Foulkes, our robber, and his two children.

Then Uncle looked at Father, and Father said, 'You tell them.'

So Uncle stood up and said, 'Children, this is important. Please listen. I'm going to live in this house. It's very big – too big for me. I asked your father and he says that you can all come and live with me. Do you want to do that? I think it will be a happy home for all of us.'

So we all went and lived with our Indian Uncle. Father's business is better now. Our friends Mrs Leslie and the robber often come to visit.

'We were the treasure-seekers,' Noel said. 'We looked for treasure, and we found a good uncle. That's the best treasure.'

EXERCISES

Vocabulary Work

Look back at the 'Dictionary Words' in this story. Do you understand them all?

1 Put these words into pairs. Then write a sentence with each pair of words.

A	B
poor	aunt
uncle	policeman
prisoner	hole
hide	guard
robber	rich
dig	find

2 Look at these words:

save	poem	princess
prison	prisoner	ground
dig	marry	idea

Three of them are *verbs*; six of them are *nouns*. Which are verbs and which are nouns? Write sentences with two or three of the words in each sentence.

Comprehension

Chapters 1–3

1 a Who is the oldest of the Bastable children?
  b Who is the youngest of the Bastable children?
  c Why do the children not like to talk about their mother?
  d Who had the idea to be robbers?

2 a Who fell in the hole in the ground?
   b What job does Albert's uncle do?
   c Who did Oswald and Noel meet in the train?

Chapters 4–6

3 a How many names did Noel's princess have?
   b How much money did the children get when they were robbers?
   c Why did Noel go red and then white in the newspaper man's office?
   d What did Pincher do to Lord Tottenham?

Chapters 7–8

4 Did you know Mr Foulkes was not a robber? How did you know?
5 Why did the children not call the police about the robber in the kitchen?
6 a Why did the Indian Uncle first visit the house?
   b Why did the children think the Indian Uncle was poor?

Discussion

1 In Chapter 5, why was Albert's uncle a little angry? Was he right?
2 In the last chapter, the children go to live with their uncle. Do you think they will be happy there? Why or why not?

Writing

1 *You* are a treasure-seeker. Write a short story. What happens? Do you find treasure? Where do you find it? How do you find it?
2 Write two or three sentences about each of the Bastable children. Which of them do you like best? Why?